Little Rat Rides

MONIKA BANG-CAMPBELL

Illustrated by MOLLY BANG

HARCOURT, INC.

Orlando   Austin   New York   San Diego   Toronto   London

With thanks to Fieldcrest Farm, Boxberry Hill Farm, Salty, and, of course, Pee Wee.

www.HarcourtBooks.com

Library of Congress Cataloging-in-Publication Data
Bang-Campbell, Monika.
Little Rat rides/Monika Bang-Campbell; illustrated by Molly Bang.
p. cm.
Summary: Little Rat overcomes her fear and learns to ride a horse, just like her daddy did when he was young.
[1. Horsemanship—Fiction. 2. Horses—Fiction. 3. Fear—Fiction. 4. Rats—Fiction.] I. Bang, Molly, ill. II. Title.
PZ7.B2218Lg 2004
[E]—dc21 2003004985
ISBN 0-15-204667-4

First edition
H G F E D C B A

Manufactured in China

The illustrations in this book were done in pencil, gouache, and watercolor, with some chalk dust, on illustration board.
The display type was set in Elroy.
The text type was set in Adobe Garamond.
Color separations by Colourscan Co. Pte. Ltd., Singapore
Manufactured by South China Printing Company, Ltd., China
This book was printed on totally chlorine-free Stora Enso Matte paper.
Production supervision by Sandra Grebenar and Pascha Gerlinger
Designed by Linda Lockowitz and Suzanne Fridley

For my father, the original Daddy Rat

—M. B-C.

Chapter 1

Daddy Rat had a photo
on his desk.
It showed a young Daddy Rat
riding his horse, Starduster,
in the Fourth of July parade.
He was wearing
a snazzy cowboy outfit
and carrying a giant American flag.
Little Rat loved looking
at that photo and hearing about
his riding adventures.
One day she said, "Daddy,
I'd like to learn to ride a horse."

So the next week,
Daddy Rat drove Little Rat
to Clodhopper Farm.
Her teacher met them at the gate.
"Hello. You must be Little Rat," she said.
"I'm Mrs. Mugpie. Your horse is waiting
for you down in the ring.
His name is Pee Wee."

As Little Rat and Daddy Rat followed
Mrs. Mugpie, a goat with a big paunch
and beady eyes came charging by.
It gave them a nasty look.
"That's Chrissy Goat," said Mrs. Mugpie.
"She's mean, but she keeps the grass mowed."

"And here is Pee Wee," Mrs. Mugpie said.
Little Rat gasped.
This was not a horse.
This was a mountain on four legs.
She hid behind Daddy Rat.
Maybe riding is not such a good idea,
she thought.
We have cars now. Why learn to ride a horse?

Chapter 2

"Pee Wee has been looking forward to meeting you, Little Rat," Mrs. Mugpie said. "But he can't see you if you're hiding."

Little Rat peeked out from behind Daddy Rat.

She looked at the saddle on Pee Wee's back. It was very high up.

Little Rat did not care for heights.

She turned to Daddy Rat and said, "I think I want to take ballet lessons instead."

"I know it's scary getting on a horse the first time," said Daddy Rat. "But Pee Wee is trained to carry beginning riders."

"And he sure likes having his nose rubbed," Mrs. Mugpie added.

Little Rat looked at Pee Wee's big head.
He seemed to be taking a snooze.
She lifted her hand.
Pee Wee lowered his head and snuffled.
Little Rat stroked his nose.
It was soft, with short prickly whiskers.
The whiskers tickled Little Rat's hand.
Pee Wee gave Little Rat a nudge
and blew on her face.
"That means he wants to take you
for a ride," said Mrs. Mugpie.
Little Rat gulped.
Her knees were shaking.
But Pee Wee *did* look awfully sweet.
"I guess I'll give it a try," Little Rat said.

Mrs. Mugpie gave her a leg up
into the saddle.
Little Rat looked down.
The ground was VERY far away.
Slowly, Mrs. Mugpie began to
lead Pee Wee around the ring.

"If you hold your arms out like an airplane,
it will help you learn to balance," Mrs. Mugpie
told Little Rat.
Pee Wee's back swayed gently.
Little Rat began to relax.
Pee Wee is old and big and fat, she thought.
He is very slow and sweet.
I think I'll come back again next week.

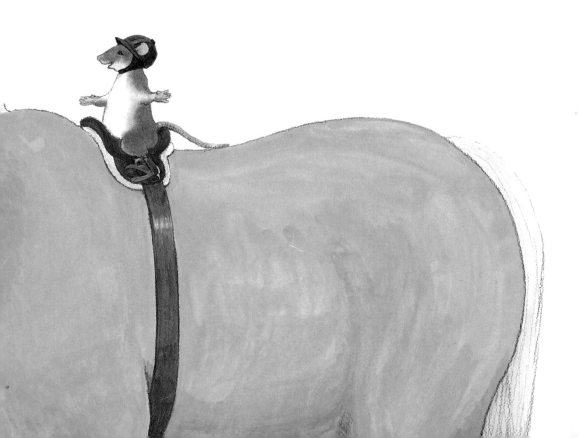

Chapter 3

Little Rat came back every week
for her lesson.
One Saturday, she was riding Pee Wee
in the indoor ring.
Suddenly, Stinker, the barn cat,
darted in front of them.
That scared the wits out of Pee Wee.
He took off around the ring.
Little Rat screamed.
She screamed very loud.
The screaming scared Pee Wee even more.
Who knew he could move so fast?

Little Rat saw
the wall of the barn
in front of her.
She thought Pee Wee
was going to smash
right into it!

She threw herself
off the saddle…

…and landed with a thud on the ground.

Little Rat was sure she was dead.
But her bum hurt a lot,
and Pee Wee was standing over her,
snorting on her head.
Mrs. Mugpie helped Little Rat to her feet.
"That was quite a tumble," she said.
"Are you ready to continue your lesson?"

Little Rat thought Mrs. Mugpie
must be joking.
She could care less about being
a fancy rider like her dad.
She was never getting on a horse again!
Little Rat started to cry.
"I know that was scary," Mrs. Mugpie said.
"But Pee Wee was scared, too.
If you get back up and ride him,
he'll feel much better."
Mrs. Mugpie helped Little Rat
get back on Pee Wee.
Then she walked around the ring
with them until Little Rat and Pee Wee
both felt safe again.

Chapter 4

After every lesson, Little Rat had to
clean Pee Wee's stall.
She got the wheelbarrow
and the giant pitchfork.
Then she set about picking
Pee Wee's poop out of his stall
and putting down fresh shavings.
Little Rat did not mind picking up
Pee Wee's poop.
But she DID mind getting the new
shavings, because mean, mean Chrissy Goat
guarded the shavings shed.
She guarded it like it was her job.

Little Rat rolled the wheelbarrow
up to the shed.
Her heart was pounding.
She peered around the door—
no sign of Chrissy Goat.
Little Rat stepped inside.
Uh-oh.
From behind the shavings pile,
two beady eyes stared out.

Before Little Rat could run,
Chrissy Goat came charging at her.
She butted Little Rat in the tummy
and knocked her down.
Little Rat was stunned for a moment,
but then she got up and ran as fast as she
could back to the barn.

Little Rat spotted Kirsten.
Kirsten had been riding forever.
She was always helpful and nice.
Little Rat told her what had happened.
"Let's go take care of that goat," Kirsten said.
Little Rat watched from outside.
She wasn't going back in there
with that goat on the loose.
Kirsten went right up to Chrissy Goat,
grabbed her horns,
and pulled her out of the shed.
Chrissy Goat gave Little Rat a nasty look
and trotted off to plan her next attack.
Kirsten helped Little Rat load up
the wheelbarrow.
Then they walked back to the barn together.

Chapter 5

After her lesson one day,
Little Rat was leading Pee Wee
back to his stall.
Pee Wee was excited about lunch.
He knew he was going to have oats and hay.
He started to trot.
Little Rat tried to make him stop.
She pulled on the reins and said,
"Whoa, Pee Wee!"
Pee Wee did stop,
but his giant hoof came
right down on her foot.
Little Rat howled.

Pee Wee didn't know he was standing
on Little Rat's foot.
He was puzzled.
Why was Little Rat howling?
He thought she must be excited
about lunch, too.
But then why were they just standing there?

Little Rat's foot hurt so much,
she forgot how to make Pee Wee move.
She tried to push him off.
She pushed his leg with all her might.
But Pee Wee was a giant horse,
and Little Rat was a little rat.
You do the math.

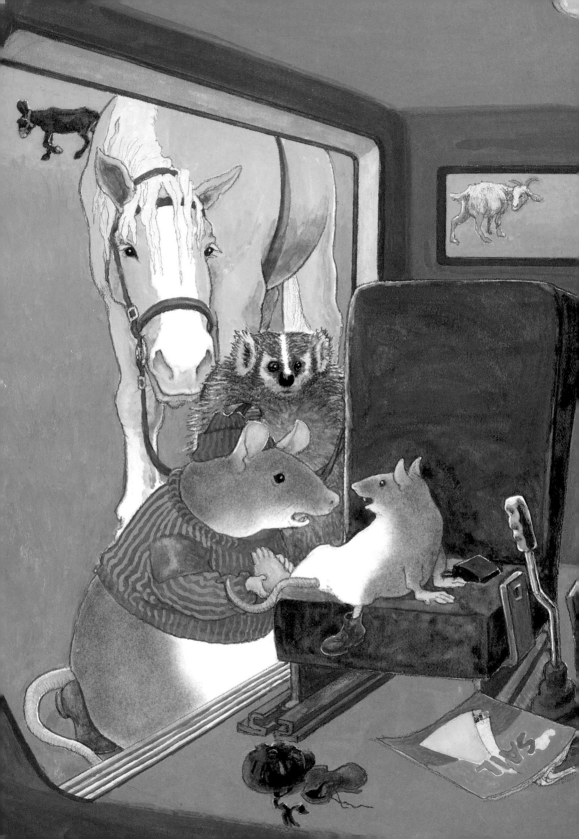

Kirsten ran over and led Pee Wee forward.
Little Rat sat down and pulled off her boot.
Her foot was puffing up like a blowfish.
Kirsten helped Little Rat limp to the truck.
Daddy Rat jumped out.
"Pee Wee stomped on my foot," Little Rat
said. "But he didn't mean to. He didn't even
know my foot was under him."
Daddy Rat picked Little Rat up
and set her on the seat.
"Can you wiggle your toes?" he asked.
"They hurt, but I can move all of them."
"That's a good sign," he said. "It means
they aren't broken."
"Great!" said Kirsten. "The Fourth of July
Horse Show is only three weeks away.
You'll be fine by then."

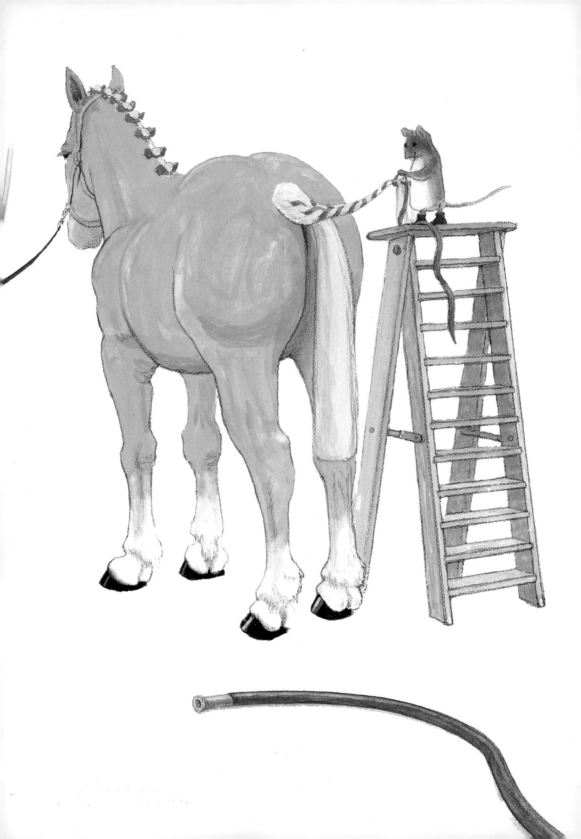

Chapter 6

Everybody at Clodhopper Farm worked
hard to get their horses ready for the show.
Little Rat gave Pee Wee a bath
with horse shampoo.
She rinsed him off and brushed his coat.
She painted his hooves with black polish.
She combed the burrs and tangles
out of his tail until it was shiny and soft.
Then she braided his mane
and tied little bows in it.
"Pee Wee," said Little Rat,
"you are a very pretty boy."

Just then, Chrissy Goat
walked into the barn.
Little Rat had nowhere to run.
She saw the hose on the ground.

She picked it up
and sprayed
Chrissy Goat.

Chrissy Goat
hightailed it out
of the barn.

"Hmph," said Little Rat.
"So much for *that* big bully."

Chapter 7

At last it was the Fourth of July,
and Little Rat was riding in the big show.
She wore a velvet helmet,
a snappy jacket, and shiny black boots.
But Little Rat was not happy.
It was a hundred degrees in the ring.
Her fur was matted to her back,
and sweat was dripping off her whiskers.
She was VERY hot and cranky.
Pee Wee was hot and cranky, too.
VERY hot and cranky.

The judge had all the
horses trot in a circle.
He watched how the
riders sat on their horses
and how they handled them.
He took notes on his clipboard.
The horses' hooves kicked up dust.
Pee Wee was having
trouble keeping up.

"You are a slowpoke,
Pee Wee," said Little Rat.
She squeezed her legs
to make him go faster,
but Pee Wee did not
pick up the pace.
Little Rat tapped
him with her crop.
Pee Wee walked faster—
for about twelve feet.

Then he stopped so suddenly that
Little Rat almost sailed over his ears.
Pee Wee's head jerked forward.
His whole body shook.
The dust in the ring had gotten
into his nose.
Pee Wee was sneezing!
A horse sneeze is a very BIG sneeze.
It felt like an earthquake.
Little Rat held on and waited
until Pee Wee had finished.
She was embarrassed.
This was not the Fourth of July Horse Show
she had dreamed about.

Finally, the show was over.
All the horses lined up
and waited for the judge.
Little Rat watched him pin
fancy ribbons on other horses' bridles.
She felt disappointed.

Then the judge was pinning a pink ribbon
on Pee Wee's bridle.
Little Rat perked up.
She and Pee Wee had won fifth prize!
Little Rat hugged Pee Wee's neck.
"I think you got a prize for sneezing,"
she told him. "That was a very
impressive display."

Chapter 8

That night after supper,
Little Rat got ready for bed.
Daddy Rat came to tuck her in.
"I am proud of you, Little Rat," he said.
"You and Pee Wee did a great job today.
Remember how nervous you were
when you first met him?"
"He was a giant, and I was scared,"
said Little Rat. "I wanted to go home."
"Why did you decide to stay?"
"Because I wanted to ride a horse
like you did," Little Rat said.
"You got bumps and bruises like I did, too,"
said Daddy Rat. "But you and Pee Wee
are a real team now."
"We sure are," said Little Rat.

"And I can't wait to ride him again tomorrow!"